This book belongs to:

____

Serafina Soars

Travel With Me • Book3

Serafina Soars

Alma Hammond

Illustrated by Anya Macleod

Book and cover design by Kelly Lenihan

ISBN: 978-1733610964 (hardcover)
ISBN: 978-1733610971 (softcover)
ISBN: 978-1733610957 (ebook)
LCCN: 2019904282

Summary: Even though Serafina is one of the mightiest birds in the sky, she is shy. Follow Serafina as she travels through Spain and discovers not only the beauty of her country, but her own self-confidence.

Bonus section includes fun facts about the animals and places in southern Spain visited in *Serafina Soars*.

JUV002360 Juvenile Fiction / Animals / Nocturnal
JUV039060 Juvenile Fiction / Social Themes / Friendship
JUV039140 Juvenile Fiction / Self-Esteem & Self-Reliance
JUV039090 Juvenile Fiction / New Experience

Produced in the United States of America

First Edition

For everyone who longs to do the things
they are a little afraid to do.

"You're off to great places,

Today is your day!

Your mountain is waiting,

So . . . get on your way!"

– Dr. Seuss

This is Serafina of Grenada, Spain. She is a Eurasian eagle owl, one of the largest owls in the world! Serafina has wide, powerful wings, which help her glide silently in the wind. Her large eyes and ear tufts help her see and hear from great distances.

Even though Serafina is one of the mightiest birds in the sky, Serafina is shy. Strange noises and sudden movements frighten her and she often feels fearful around others.

Serafina mostly keeps to herself, and is only active at night when her surroundings are much quieter. Deep inside, Serafina longs to build her confidence so she can enjoy more of life.

One evening, Serafina was startled by the sounds of a Spanish classical guitar, accompanied by humans singing, clapping, and stomping to loud flamenco music.

Resisting the urge to hide, she decided to satisfy her curiosity and seek the source of the soulful sounds.

The music led her to a square where Flamenco dancers were moving with strong emotion to a spirited song set to strummed guitar music. Shy Serafina kept her distance, landing in a tree away from the crowd.

"Hey! What are you doing up there?" cried a donkey, "Are you scared? Come closer! Scaredy pants! Scaredy pants!" he taunted.

Serafina, feeling embarrassed, flew off in a hurry, landing on a fountain in an old palace called The Alhambra.

Two turtle doves landed on the fountain next to her. Tempted to fly away, their soft purr persuaded her to stay awhile.

"Turrrrr, turrrr. Hi there," said one of the turtle doves.

"Hi," replied Serafina shyly.

"I saw what happened at the square," said the turtle dove. "Don't feel bad. That old donkey doesn't like himself, so he bullies others. I wouldn't worry about him."

Serafina considered the bird's words. "Thank you," she said.

Just then, the loud clanging of nearby church bells startled Serafina, and she took off into the night sky. As she flew over the source of the noise, two Iberian white storks called out to her, "Hey there. Come join us!"

"But the bells? They are so loud!" cried Serafina.

"They will stop soon," said the storks.

With the last clang of the bells, Serafina landed on top of the cathedral next to the two storks.

"It's a beautiful night!" chirped one of the storks.

TAPTAP
TAPTAP
TAPTAP

"Yes, it is," said Serafina. "But how can you stand living here with those bells going off all the time?"

"Oh, that? It used to bother us, but it really doesn't anymore. In fact, we've come to like it."

Serafina remained with the storks for several more moments, taking in the beauty of the town at night. Then she returned to her roost in the forest, feeling exhausted from her day but somehow stronger inside.

Serafina's adventures from the night before gave her the courage to fly out into the sunlight, something she had never done before.

Now each day, well before dusk, Serafina flies somewhere new: over miles of olive trees, hilltop castles, and amazing places built hundreds of years ago.

One day she flew to the very tip of southern Spain where she spied one of the largest rocks in the world, the Rock of Gibraltar. There she met up with a rowdy group of Barbary macaque monkeys. Watching closely as they played together, Serafina called out to them, "Oohu-oohu-oohu, hellooooooo?"

One of the monkeys stopped his game to grunt back with a grin.

Serafina spent the day with the monkeys, watching them play, feeling safe and happy.

Today, Serafina flies farther and farther to places she has never seen before.

Venturing out to explore the beauty of her country and be with others makes Serafina's spirit soar!

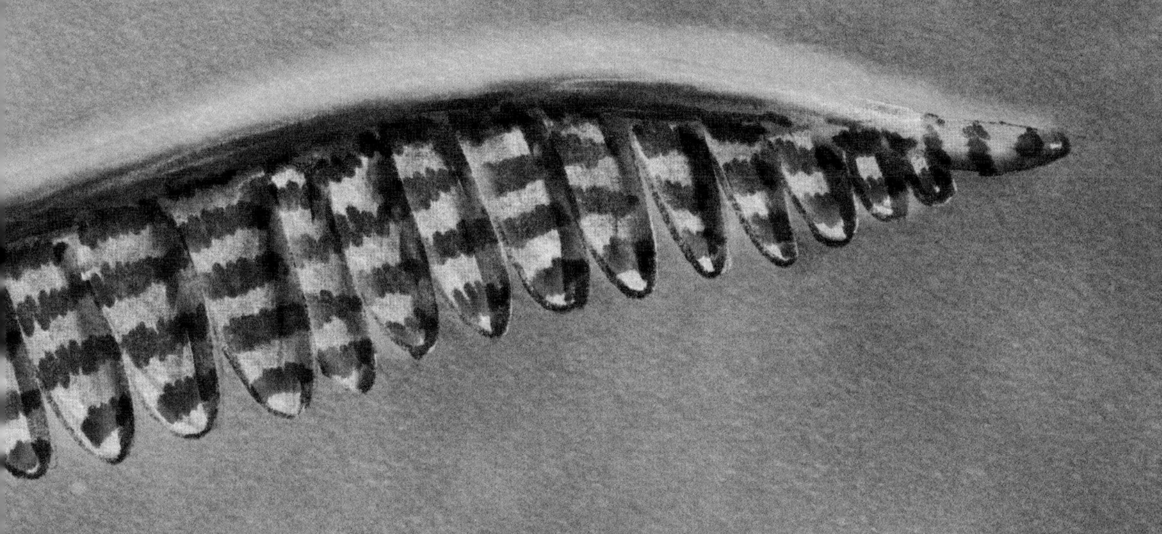

Fun Facts

Eurasian Eagle Owl (*Bubo bubo*)

- The eagle owl is one of the largest of owl species. Females can grow up to 30 inches long with a wingspan of 6 foot 2 inches. Males are smaller.
- The eagle owl call to protect their territory is "Oohu-oohu-oohu," which they repeat every 10 seconds.
- Eagle owls tend to live alone, are mostly nocturnal, and are most active at dawn and dusk.

Flamenco Dancing

- Flamenco music is popular all over Spain but can be traced back to Andalucia, a southern region of Spain that includes Seville, Grenada, Malaga, Gibraltar, and other smaller towns.
- Arabic, Andalusia, Sephardic, and gypsy cultures combined to create what is known as the Flamenco dance.
- Flamenco is also called *baile* which means "dance" in Spanish.

Donkey (*Equus asinus*)

- Donkeys have a reputation for being stubbon. In fact, they are cautious animals and won't move ahead if they are fearful.
- Donkeys make a loud, braying noise that goes on for several seconds. It sounds like "Hee-haw, hee-haw."
- Donkeys are related to horses and zebras.

European Turtle Dove (*Treptopelia turtur*)

- The turtle dove gets its name from the sound it makes, "Turr, turr." There is no connection to its name and the reptile.
- A pair of turtle doves symbolize love and peace.
- Pet turtle doves can live 20 years or more.

The Alhambra Palace / Fountain of Lions

- The palace is very old. It started off as a small fort built in 899 in Andalusia, Spain and was converted to a royal palace in 1333 by the Sultan of Grenada.
- The palace was home to Moorish royal families until 1492 when Catholics again regained rule of Spain.
- The Fountain of the Lions is a famous fountain located in the middle of the Alhambra in the Courtyard of Lions. It is part of a complex water system, which enables a constant flow of water throughout the interior and exterior of the palace.

Iberian White Stork (*Ciconia ciconia*)

- White storks make a loud clattering sound by opening and closing their beaks quickly: "Tap, tap, tap."
- The white stork is famous for building its stick nests on top of buildings, cathedrals, and other structures, when it can't find trees suitable for nesting.
- The white stork symbolizes mercy and kindness, and its image appears on more than 120 different postage stamps around the world.

The Grenada Cathedral

- Construction of the Cathedral, located in Grenada began in 1523.
- The Cathedral is a work of art, with fancy architecture, doors, paintings, windows, and sculptures.
- Thousands of visitors come to see the Grenada cathedral each year.

The Rock of Gibraltar

- The rock of Gibraltar is made of limestone and is 426 meters (465 yards) high.
- It is located in the British territory of Gibraltar near the southwestern tip of Spain.
- About 315 species of birds pass over Gibraltar, many of which are migratory.

Barbary Macaque Monkey (*Macaca sylvanus*)

- There are over 250 Barbary macaques living on the rock of Gibraltar in southern Spain.
- Barbary macaques have large cheek pouches which can hold as much food as their stomachs.
- Macaques help each other to raise their young.

Thank you for adding *Serafina Soars* to your library.

If your child enjoys this story, please consider posting a thoughtful review on Amazon or Goodreads on your child's behalf.

Your kindness will make a difference for other readers considering this book.

In gratitude,

Alma

The author with the inspiration for Serafina Soars, *an eagle owl she encountered on a trip to Spain in 2018.*

Hi Kids,

Send me a letter or draw me a picture. I'd love to hear from you!

Alma

Alma Hammond

P.O. Box 30921

Chevy Chase, MD 20815

U.S.A.

Happy reading!

Meet the Author

Alma Hammond is the award-winning author of five picture books for children. In her Travel With Me series, children meet and learn about the animals and places of the countries Alma has visited. The stories celebrate friendship, diversity, respect for nature, and acceptance of others and self. All of Alma's children's books are written to educate and entertain both the adult and child, and are inspired by fascinating discoveries about life.

Alma lives with her husband Bob, dog Stazi, and two cats Violet and Daisy, in Bethesda, MD. When Alma is not writing, she enjoys yoga, cooking, and traveling. Learn more about Alma and what she's working on by visiting sweetbeetbooks.com

Other books in the Travel With Me series
Book One: *Super Rooster and Wonder Cat* (Bora Bora, Tahiti),
Book Two: *André the Five-Star Cat* (Paris, France).
Available on Amazon and other online outlets and by request from your favorite bookstore or library.

Meet the Illustrator

Anya McLeod has been drawing and painting since she was a very young child, using a variety of mediums including watercolors, acrylics and charcoal. Her inspiration comes from nature, with animals, the ocean, and plant life being some of her favorite subjects.

Anya was born in Russia, moving with her family when she was only eight. She now lives in Adelaide, Australia with her husband, daughter, giant dog and cat. This is her second children's book illustration project, and she plans to continue with both fiction and non-fiction illustrations. When Anya is not illustrating, she enjoys camping, cooking and anything creative!

Made in the USA
Middletown, DE
16 July 2019